The SONG *Within My* HEART

Nokum Relaxing, 51 cm × 41 cm (20" × 16"), 2000

The SONG *Within My* HEART

Paintings by ALLEN SAPP

Story by DAVID BOUCHARD

RAINCOAST BOOKS

Vancouver

Listen to the beating drum
It tells a hundred stories
Of our people, of our homeland
Some of birds and beasts and sweet grass.

Close your eyes and listen
You might come to hear a story
That no one hears but you alone
A story of your very own.

BOOM boom boom boom BOOM boom boom boom
BOOM boom boom boom BOOM boom boom boom.
BOOM boom boom boom BOOM boom boom boom
BOOM boom boom boom BOOM boom boom boom.

The Man Singing While She's Doing Beads, 61 cm × 46 cm (24" × 18"), 1990

Listen to the singers
They are also telling stories
Some of pleasure, some of sorrow
Some of birth or life here after.

Close your eyes and listen
You might come to hear a story
That no one hears but you alone
Another of your very own.

An Indoor Pow-Wow, 46 cm × 61 cm (18" × 24"), 1995

HEY hey hey hey Hi hey hey hey   HI hey hey hey HEY hey hi.

HEY hey hey hey Hi hey hey hey HI hey hey hey HEY hey hey!

I'm Watching Nokum Feed the Chickens, 46 cm × 46 cm (18" × 18"), 2001

When at first I heard them

I was standing near my Nokum

I stood staring at my elder

Who was lost somewhere in deepest thought.

When at first I heard them
I was standing with my Nokum
Who smiled and began swaying
Closed her eyes and started singing.
Not loud at first, a simple hum
I tugged with force on both her arms.

This Is A Pow-Wow, 61 cm × 91 cm (24" × 36"), 2000

"Grandma," I called out to her
"I don't know what they're saying!"
She couldn't or she didn't hear
Yet I was loud and she was near.

"Grandma," I yelled out again
"Please tell me what they're saying."
She smiled as she looked down at me
And taught me how to hear and see.

HEY hey hey hey Hi hey hey hey
HI hey hey hey HEY hey hi.

HEY hey hey hey Hi hey hey hey
HI hey hey hey HEY hey hey!

They Will Be Drummers One Day, 61 cm × 61 cm (24" × 24"), 1995

Nokum Is Peeling Potatoes, 46 cm × 46 cm (18" × 18"), 2001

"Child," she said, "There are some things
That you can call your very own.
Not toys or clothes, not jewels or cars
Don't ever make these things your own."

"There aren't a lot but there *are* things
That you should learn to call your own.
Your stories, songs and beating heart
Are truly yours and yours alone."

HEY hey hey hey Hi hey hey hey
HI hey hey hey HEY hey hi.

HEY hey hey hey Hi hey hey hey
HI hey hey hey HEY hey hey!

Nokum Making Bannock Outside, 30 cm × 41 cm (12" × 16"), 1989

And right there at that pow-wow

(Nokum knew the time for teaching)

The scorching sun echoed the drums

The dancers would be soon to come.

"Yes child," she said, "There are some things

That you can call your very own.

Your stories, songs and beating heart

Are truly yours and yours alone."

HEY hey hey hey Hi hey hey hey
        HI hey hey hey HEY hey hi.

                HEY hey hey hey Hi hey hey hey
                        HI hey hey hey HEY hey hey!

At The Pow-Wow, 30 cm × 41 cm (12" × 16"), 1985

HEY hey hey hey

Hi hey hey hey

HI hey hey hey

HEY hey hi.

HEY hey hey hey

Hi hey hey hey

HI hey hey hey

HEY hey hey!

Summer Pow-Wow, 61 cm × 91 cm (24" × 36"), 2002

"A story is a sacred thing
That should be passed from age to youth
I choose to share my best with you
That you might own and share them too."

"And never use another's tale
Unless he knows and he approves.
And only then and then alone
Might you tell it to others."

Ceremony To Remember Someone, 76 cm × 122 cm (30" × 48"), 2001

HEY hey hey hey Hi hey hey hey   HI hey hey hey HEY hey hi.

HEY hey hey hey Hi hey hey hey HI hey hey hey HEY hey hey!

"And much the same, the beating drum
It echoes that which is your soul
You seek a rhythm that is true
Of all the secrets that are you.

"So much of what the drummer feels
Is clear with every beat you hear.
He bares it all, he cannot hide.
He's sharing what he is inside."

BOOM boom boom boom BOOM boom boom boom
BOOM boom boom boom BOOM boom boom.
BOOM boom boom boom BOOM boom boom boom
BOOM boom boom boom BOOM boom boom.

The Man Is Going To Sing A Song, 41 cm × 30 cm (16" × 12"), 1992

My Grandmother Telling A Story, 30 cm × 41 cm (12" × 16"), 1987

"And of the things in my own life
    That I have owned, there are none so dear
    As songs I sing and stories tell
    All tales that you should know by now.

"To understand the song I sing
    Close your eyes and listen
    And try to hear the subtle things
    It is your Nokum's heart that sings."

HEY hey hey hey Hi hey hey hey
        HI hey hey hey HEY hey hi.

HEY hey hey hey Hi hey hey hey
        HI hey hey hey HEY hey hey!

If you, dear reader, hear me sing
And can't make out my message
You should not fret, I was like you
I had to learn to listen too!

To understand the song I sing
Close your eyes and listen
And try to hear the subtle things
It's of my Nokum that I sing.

HEY hey hey hey Hi hey hey hey
HI hey hey hey HEY hey hi.

HEY hey hey hey Hi hey hey hey
HI hey hey hey HEY hey hey!

Nokum's Tender Love, 61 cm × 46 cm (24" × 18"), 2002

A note from the painter

I like to go to pow-wows and experience the renewal of soul and body which happens there. Pow-wows are a time of happiness with the songs telling a story and the dancers adding to the excitement. Dancing with other people from near and far brings me closer to my people. This is a time for young and old to get together in friendship and happiness.

Our old people have much to teach us if we will only listen. In my own life I remember with deep gratitude the influence my Nokum — my grandmother — had on me. I liked to draw while I was in school and sometimes the teacher would hand out one of my drawings as a prize for the rest of the children. One time I asked Nokum if I could draw her and she said, "Sure, go ahead and do it." She told me that if I kept at my drawing I would be very happy some day. And I remember her words of advice: "Don't do stupid things, like getting involved with alcohol and drugs."

My Nokum, Maggie Soonias

I have often painted my Nokum making bannock, feeding the chickens or doing bead work. I would help her feed the chickens and go into the hen house to gather up eggs. I only went to school for a short time and although I never learned to read and write my Nokum and my father Alex taught me to show respect, not only for the people but for everything that Manito has put on the earth. That is why when we go to pow-wows to dance we also offer thanks to the good earth, the animals, the birds and nature, which provides for all of our needs. I am happy that for thirty years I have been able to paint scenes from my childhood on the reserve and share the beauty that Manito has created with all people.

Me (second from left) with my father Alex and my sister and three brothers

Parents and grandparents must teach young people the important things in life and help to preserve our culture so that Indian people will be proud of their heritage. My father said I should thank Manito as I wake in the morning and before I go to sleep at night. He used to sing to me and one of my fondest memories is when he took me to my first pow-wow and while resting on his shoulders I heard the beat of the drums. He also encouraged me to let my hair grow long, to show people that I was a *Naheyow*, an Indian.

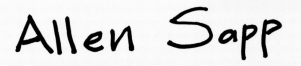

Allen Sapp

To Maggie Soonias, who encouraged me to paint and inspired me to do my best.

Artwork copyright © 2002 by Allen Sapp
Text copyright © 2002 by David Bouchard

Edited by Scott Steedman
Designed by Ingrid Paulson

Raincoast Books
9050 Shaughnessy Street
Vancouver, British Columbia
Canada, V6P 6E5
www.raincoast.com

In the United States:
Publishers Group West
1700 Fourth Street
Berkeley, California
94710

Raincoast Books is a member of CANCOPY (Canadian Copyright Licensing Agency). No part of this publication may be reproduced, stored in a retrieval system or transmitted in any form or by any means without prior written permission from the publisher, or, in case of photocopying or other reprographic copying, a license from CANCOPY, One Yonge Street, Toronto, Ontario, M5E 1E5.

Raincoast Books acknowledges the ongoing financial support of the Government of Canada through The Canada Council for the Arts and the Book Publishing Industry Development Program (BPIDP); and the Government of British Columbia through the BC Arts Council.

NATIONAL LIBRARY OF CANADA CATALOGUING IN PUBLICATION DATA
Bouchard, Dave, 1952–
    Song, within my heart, The

    ISBN 1-55192-559-1

    I. Sapp, Allen, 1929- II. Title.

PS8553.O759 S66 2002   jC813'.54   C2002-910553-6
PZ7.B682So 2002

LIBRARY OF CONGRESS CONTROL NUMBER: 2002091845

Printed and bound in Hong Kong by
Book Art Inc.,Toronto

1 2 3 4 5 6 7 8 9 10

ACKNOWLEDGEMENTS
"Thank you John, Monica and James Kurtz, my good friends and manager for many years." — A.S.
"I would like to acknowledge the presence and contribution of my friend James Kurtz, the late son of John and Monica Kurtz. James was so present in so much of this." — D.B.